Fluffy

By Jody Perkins

First Printing: 2016

ISBN-13: 978-1532870118

ISBN-10: 1532870116

Fluffy:

– a bunny's tale

Fluffy was an adorable bunny. He had long white fur, long fuzzy ears, a fluffy round tail, big black eyes and a cute pink nose.

He really got his name from his tail, because it was so soft and "fluffy".

He was a happy bunny. You see, he had a beautiful mother whose name was Janel, and a handsome father whose name was Tory.

He also had a sister named Tina and a brother named Sid.

Now, they all lived in a very comfortable rabbit hole on the side of a lovely green hill.

There was a family of people who lived at the top of the hill. There was a mother, a father, a little girl named Jessie and a little boy named Josh.

The children went to school each day. On their way they always stopped to pat the bunnies and give them some carrots.

Sometimes Tina, Sid and Fluffy would wander off into the next yard where there was a big garden. They especially liked the nice green lettuce that they found there. Once in a while they would chomp on some cabbage leaves and carrot tops as well.

Of course, this did not make the farmer very happy and he would shoo them out with a rake.

If Tina couldn't hop as fast as Sid and Fluffy, she would hide under a squash leaf until the farmer went inside. Then she would eat some more lettuce before going home.

Her mother wondered many times why Tina would not eat her supper, until one day Sid and Fluffy told her what Tina had eaten. The mother really corrected Tina and told the bunnies never to go into anyone's garden again because that was stealing someone else's food.

Tina had never thought of it that way before, so she decided to be good.

Fluffy and Sid said they would also be good and stay in their own yard.

After all, the little boy and girl who lived up the hill fed them very well every day.

One day some builders came to town and started clearing some land to build houses. Of course, they didn't know the rabbit family lived in a rabbit hole on the hill and they completely covered the entrance to their home.

They would never have gotten out, except that Jessie and Josh saw what had happened. They asked their father to help them get the bunnies out. They worked fast and furious and reached the bunnies just in time to save their lives.

They took Tina, Sid, Fluffy and their parents, Janel and Tory, up to their house. The children's parents built a lovely large wooden house for them.

They attached a wire pen so the family of bunnies could go outside. Now this wasn't quite like their cozy rabbit hole, but they were so happy to be safe and sound.

Every day the children brought fresh water and carrots and lettuce for the bunnies. What a nice family they were!

Fluffy was the largest of all the bunnies and he grew into a beautiful rabbit. I think he was the children's favorite one, but they were good to all of them.

Now Jessie and Josh also had a very large dog. His name was Dane.

Under the rabbit hutch made a great place for Dane to curl up in the shade and be nice and cool.

He also felt like he was guarding the rabbit family and that made him feel very important.

He also kept his eyes and ears on the family's home because they were a very special family.

About the Book

1. How many butterflies can you find?

2. How many dragonflies can you find?

3. Can you find a four leaf clover?

4. Can you find a frog?

5. Can you find the half-eaten carrot that Fluffy is hiding?

About the Book

Answers:

1. Four

2. Six (if you count the one on the cover)

3. Page 11

4. Page 11

5. Page 11

About the Author

Jody was born and raised in Amesbury, Massachusetts. Her given name was Joanne, but when she was in Junior High School, her friends decided to call her Jody – and it stuck.

Many years ago she took a course in Children's Literature at a local college. She wrote a few children's stories, but shortly after, tragedy struck her family and she had to stop writing.

Now many years later, she is "back on track" and hoping her stories will make children happy.

About the Illustrator

David Shaw's career was in education for many years, serving as an elementary teacher and on up to principal of two schools. In the art field he has illustrated a manual for a speech prosthesis called Mr. Big Mouth. He has done a number of coloring books including one on Fire Safety for elementary school training. He did a calendar of historical buildings for his town and has a series of note cards that includes those illustrations among other things. He has also illustrated eight poetry books and four children's books.

Other Stories by Jody Perkins

The Little Frog That Wasn't

This is a children's story of a blue frog who dreamed of being green

The Little Green Man

This is a children's story of a lonely green man who befriends a cat with green eyes and a beautiful green parakeet.

Made in the USA
Middletown, DE
30 November 2016

37554361R00021